Grace Unmeasured

The Hope Series, Volume 4

Colton Lee

Published by Colton Lee, 2024.

This is a work of fiction. Similarities to real people, places, or events are entirely coincidental.

GRACE UNMEASURED

First edition. December 5, 2024.

ISBN: 979-8230637493

Written by Colton Lee.

Table of Contents

Prologue

The valley rested in an uneasy quiet, the morning sun stretching tentative rays across the ruins of the battlefield. The fortress, once a towering monument to oppression, now lay in jagged heaps of stone, a grim reminder of the chains they had broken. Yet, as Emmalyn Calder looked out over the wreckage, victory felt less like triumph and more like exhaustion.

She stood at the edge of the ridge, her arms folded tightly across her chest. The wind tugged at her cloak, carrying with it the mingling scents of earth and ash. Her mechanical arm hummed faintly as she flexed its fingers, a restless habit she'd developed in the weeks since the battle ended.

Annabeth Calder sat a few paces behind her, cross-legged in the tall grass. Her head was bowed, lips moving in silent prayer. She had always been the steady one, the hopeful one. But even Annabeth felt the lingering shadows of doubt clinging to their victory.

"I don't know how you keep doing that," Emmalyn muttered without turning.

Annabeth looked up, blinking at her sister's back. "Doing what?"

"Praying like it's going to change anything." Emmalyn turned, her expression guarded but her tone edged with frustration. "We won, Annabeth. The chains are gone, the fortress is dust... but look around. The world's still a mess. People are still suffering. Where's the change we fought for?"

Annabeth rose to her feet, brushing her hands on her tunic. "Maybe the change doesn't happen all at once," she said softly. "Maybe it's something we grow into. Something we have to nurture."

Emmalyn scoffed, shaking her head. "That sounds a lot like 'just keep waiting.' We've been waiting long enough."

Annabeth stepped closer, her gaze steady and unwavering. "It's not about waiting. It's about trusting. There's a difference."

"Trusting in what?" Emmalyn asked, her voice rising slightly. "That if we keep stumbling forward, everything will magically get better?"

Annabeth hesitated, her brow furrowing. She didn't have an easy answer, but her heart burned with the conviction that there was still something more—something worth pressing toward.

Before she could speak, a sound rose from the valley below. It was faint at first, like the rustling of leaves, but it grew steadily, becoming a low, resonant hum that seemed to vibrate through the ground.

Both sisters turned toward the ruins, their eyes narrowing as the sound swelled. The broken stones seemed to shimmer in the sunlight, their jagged edges catching the light in ways that defied reason.

"What is that?" Emmalyn asked, her hand instinctively moving to the hilt of her sword.

Annabeth took a hesitant step forward, her breath catching in her throat. "It sounds like... singing."

Emmalyn frowned. "Singing? From where?"

"I don't know," Annabeth whispered, her voice filled with wonder. "But it feels... alive. Like it's coming from the earth itself."

As the sound washed over them, Annabeth felt a stirring deep within her—a warmth that spread through her chest and chased away the lingering chill of doubt. She couldn't explain it, but the sound didn't frighten her. It filled her with an unfamiliar, fragile hope.

Emmalyn, on the other hand, was less convinced. She drew her sword, her mechanical fingers tightening around the hilt. "If this is some kind of trap, I'm not letting it catch us off guard."

"It's not a trap," Annabeth said, her voice firm despite the uncertainty of her words. "It's a call. Can't you feel it?"

Emmalyn hesitated, her grip loosening slightly as she studied her sister's face. There was something unshakable in Annabeth's eyes—something that hadn't been there before.

"I don't feel anything except tired," Emmalyn said finally.

Annabeth smiled faintly. "Maybe that's because you're still carrying it all by yourself."

The hum softened, fading into the wind, but its presence lingered, a quiet echo in the back of their minds.

Annabeth turned toward the distant mountains, her gaze sharpening. "We're not done yet, Em."

Emmalyn's brow furrowed. "What are you talking about? The fortress is gone. The chains are broken. What else is there?"

Annabeth looked back at her, her expression calm but resolute. "There are more chains out there—ones we can't see. Fear. Doubt. Hopelessness. If we stop now, who's going to show the world that those can be broken too?"

Emmalyn let out a slow breath, the weight of her sister's words settling on her shoulders. She hated how right Annabeth always seemed to be, even when it meant facing something she didn't want to acknowledge.

"And you think marching off to... wherever is going to fix all that?" Emmalyn asked, gesturing vaguely toward the horizon.

"I think we've seen what happens when we give up," Annabeth replied. "And I think it's worth trying to build something better."

For a long moment, neither of them spoke. The wind shifted, carrying the scent of wildflowers and fresh earth—a small but undeniable promise of renewal.

Finally, Emmalyn sighed, sheathing her sword. "Fine. But don't expect me to start praying anytime soon."

Annabeth grinned, the light in her eyes growing brighter. "You don't have to. Just walk with me."

And so, they set off toward the mountains, the ruins of the fortress fading into the distance behind them. The path ahead was uncertain, but with each step, Annabeth's faith grew steadier, and even Emmalyn felt a faint spark of hope stirring within her.

The world wasn't fixed. The journey wasn't over. But as the sun climbed higher into the sky, the sisters walked forward—not in fear, but in quiet, growing faith that the story wasn't finished yet.

Signs of the End

The air in the camp was heavy, not with despair, but with the weight of anticipation. The small fire crackled weakly, its light flickering against the jagged rocks that surrounded the group like sentinels. The sisters sat among the others they had gathered during their journey—survivors, warriors, and those whose faith had been kindled by the battles they had fought.

Noah crouched by the fire, sharpening his blade with slow, deliberate strokes. The rhythmic scrape of metal against stone was the only sound for a time, broken occasionally by the distant howling of the wind.

"We're close," Annabeth said softly, her gaze fixed on the horizon.

Emmalyn glanced up from where she sat, her mechanical hand resting on her knee. "Close to what?"

Annabeth's voice didn't waver. "To the end. The signs are all around us. We're nearing the end of the seven years."

At her words, the group grew quiet, each person turning inward to consider the weight of what she had said.

"The end," Noah muttered, his voice tinged with both hope and unease. "You mean the return of Christ."

Annabeth nodded, her expression filled with quiet certainty. "That's what He promised. 'For as lightning that comes from the east is visible even in the west, so will be the coming of the Son of Man.' The signs are everywhere—the wars, the famine, the darkness that's tried to consume the world. But through it all, the faithful have endured. He's coming. I can feel it."

Emmalyn leaned back, her brow furrowed. "I don't doubt you, Annabeth, but we've been walking through this for years. Signs or not, it's hard to believe that relief is just around the corner."

Kelli, seated cross-legged across from them, spoke up. "She's right, though. I've been keeping track. The timeline matches what the scriptures said. Seven years of tribulation. Seven years of suffering. We've faced every seal, every trumpet, and every bowl of wrath."

"Then why does it still feel like we're in the middle of it?" Emmalyn asked, her tone sharper than she intended.

"Because we are," Wheels interjected, his voice calm but firm. The older man leaned forward in his chair, his weathered face lit by the fire. "The seventh year isn't over yet. And we all know the final days will be the hardest."

Annabeth clasped her hands tightly in her lap. "But they'll also bring the greatest hope. The scriptures say that when the world reaches its darkest hour, the heavens will open, and the King will return. We have to hold on."

Noah snorted softly. "Hold on, huh? That's easy to say when you've got hope left. Some of us..." He trailed off, his eyes shadowed.

"You're still here, Noah," Annabeth said gently. "That means you've got more faith than you think. God hasn't forgotten us."

For a moment, no one spoke. The crackle of the fire seemed louder in the stillness.

Finally, Kelli broke the silence. "The real question is—what do we do now? We're not just going to sit here and wait, are we?"

Annabeth shook her head. "No. We're going to keep moving. There's still work to be done. Every soul we meet, every person we bring back to the light, is a victory. We can't stop now."

"And what happens if we don't make it?" Emmalyn asked, her voice quiet.

Annabeth turned to her sister, her expression filled with a strength that seemed to glow from within. "Then we keep going anyway. Because even if we don't see Him with our own eyes, we'll know we did what we were called to do. That's what matters."

Wheels nodded slowly, his gaze thoughtful. "The battle isn't just about surviving. It's about being ready. We fight not because we're strong, but because we know Who fights for us."

The words settled over the group like a balm, quieting their doubts, if only for a moment.

Noah sighed, standing and sheathing his blade. "Well, if we're going to keep moving, we'd better get some rest while we can. Something tells me we're going to need it."

The group murmured their agreement, each person retreating to their own thoughts as they prepared for another day of uncertainty.

Emmalyn lingered by the fire, watching as the flames danced in the cool night air. Annabeth sat beside her, silent for a time before speaking.

"You're scared," Annabeth said softly.

Emmalyn didn't deny it. "You're not?"

Annabeth smiled faintly. "Of course I am. But fear doesn't get the final say. He does."

Emmalyn looked at her sister, her expression unreadable. "Do you really think we'll see Him? That we'll be there when it happens?"

"I don't just think it," Annabeth said, her voice steady. "I believe it."

For the first time that night, Emmalyn felt a flicker of something she hadn't felt in a long time. It wasn't certainty, and it wasn't peace. But it was enough to keep her moving forward.

As the fire burned low and the stars filled the sky, the group rested, their hearts heavy but their faith quietly growing. They didn't know what the next days would bring, but they knew this: the end of the story wasn't theirs to write. It was His.

And in that truth, they found the strength to carry on.

Gathering Storms

The morning broke with an unnatural stillness, the kind that felt like the world was holding its breath. The sky, streaked with angry reds and purples, hung heavy over the horizon, where a dark mass of clouds churned like a living thing. Emmalyn Calder stood at the edge of their camp, her sharp eyes scanning the horizon. Something was coming. She could feel it.

Behind her, the camp buzzed with quiet preparation. The survivors, now calling themselves the *Chain Breakers*, moved with purpose, their faces lined with determination and exhaustion. Their numbers had grown over the months as their mission expanded—rescuing the lost and restoring hope in the broken. But even with their resolve, they all felt the weight of what lay ahead.

Annabeth moved through the camp, offering calm words and quiet prayers to those who needed it. She stopped beside Wheels, who was meticulously adjusting the crossbow strapped to his chair.

"Do you feel it?" she asked softly.

Wheels nodded, his expression grim. "Hard not to. Feels like the calm before a storm."

"It's more than that," Annabeth said, her voice trembling slightly. "Something is stirring. I think this is it, Wheels. The battle we've been waiting for."

He looked up at her, his weathered face betraying no fear, only resolve. "Then we'd better make sure we're ready."

Across the camp, Kelli tightened the straps on her armor, her axe gleaming in the morning light. Noah leaned against a tree nearby, his spear balanced casually in his hand, but his eyes were sharp, scanning the horizon for any sign of movement.

"You think Roland's finally making his move?" Kelli asked, breaking the silence.

Noah shrugged, his voice low. "He has to. He's running out of time. If the timeline is right, Christ's return is close. If Roland wants to make his stand, it's now or never."

"And we're the ones standing in his way," Kelli said, her tone grim.

"That's what we signed up for, isn't it?" Noah replied, a faint smirk tugging at the corner of his mouth.

Kelli's laughter was dry. "Not exactly what I had in mind when I joined up, but here we are."

At the center of camp, Emmalyn stood with Annabeth and Wheels, a map of the region spread across a makeshift table. The ruined cities and desolate plains marked on the parchment told the story of a world ravaged by tribulation.

"Reports say Roland's forces are gathering near Megiddo," Wheels said, tracing a line with his finger. "It's the perfect location—elevated ground, strategic positioning. And..." He hesitated, his voice lowering. "The scriptures call it Armageddon."

Annabeth nodded solemnly. "The final battle."

Emmalyn frowned, her mechanical fingers tapping the table. "How many?"

"Too many," Wheels admitted. "His army is vast, filled with those who've taken the mark. And worse—those who've been deceived into thinking Roland's the answer."

"We can't let them win," Annabeth said, her voice steady despite the fear flickering in her eyes.

"We won't," Emmalyn replied firmly. "But we need a plan. We're not walking into this blind."

Noah joined them, his spear resting against his shoulder. "We're going to need more than a plan. Roland's not just building an army—he's preparing for a war on a scale the world's never seen. If the Anti-Christ is with him..." He trailed off, the weight of his words sinking in.

Kelli approached, her expression serious. "We don't just need a strategy. We need faith. If we try to fight this on our own, we'll lose before we even begin."

Annabeth placed a hand on her sister's shoulder. "She's right, Em. This isn't just a physical battle. It's spiritual. Every person who stands with Roland is someone who's been blinded by the enemy. If we're going to fight, we have to do it with more than weapons."

Emmalyn's jaw tightened, but she nodded. "Then we fight with everything we have—our strength, our faith, and whatever grace God gives us."

The sky darkened further, the churning clouds seeming to stretch closer to the earth. A distant rumble of thunder echoed across the plains, and with it came the unmistakable sound of marching.

Noah climbed a nearby ridge, his eyes narrowing as he peered into the distance. "They're coming," he called out, his voice carrying over the camp.

The *Chain Breakers* turned as one, their movements swift and purposeful. Armor was fastened, weapons were drawn, and prayers were whispered as they prepared for what was to come.

Annabeth stepped beside Emmalyn, her voice quiet but firm. "Whatever happens, we stand together. We've come too far to fall apart now."

Emmalyn glanced at her sister, a faint smile breaking through her determined expression. "You're not getting rid of me that easily."

The two sisters turned toward the horizon, where the dark mass of Roland's forces began to emerge—a sea of black banners and twisted figures marching with terrifying precision. At the center of the army rode Roland, his face calm and cruel, his presence radiating authority.

Behind him, the Anti-Christ loomed, a figure of pure malice cloaked in shadow. Even from a distance, the *Chain Breakers* could feel the oppressive weight of his presence.

Wheels rolled to Emmalyn's side, his crossbow loaded and ready. "This is it. The battle to end all battles."

"No," Annabeth said, her voice carrying a quiet power that made everyone pause. "This isn't the end. It's the beginning. And no matter how dark it gets, we're not alone."

As the first rays of sunlight broke through the storm clouds, illuminating the battlefield, the *Chain Breakers* took their positions.

The time for waiting was over. The battle had begun.

One Voice

The battlefield stretched vast and barren, its cracked earth littered with the scars of the tribulation years. Opposing armies gathered at the edges of this desolate plain, their banners fluttering in the wind that carried whispers of war. On one side stood Roland's legions, dark and imposing, a sea of black armor and sharpened steel. At the forefront, the Anti-Christ sat astride a midnight steed, his presence like a suffocating shadow, his eyes gleaming with malice.

On the other side stood the *Chain Breakers*. Smaller in number, their armor was patched, their weapons well-worn. But their eyes burned with something Roland's forces could never understand: hope. They stood shoulder to shoulder, each one ready to lay down their life for a cause far greater than themselves.

Emmalyn walked the line, her sword resting on her shoulder, her mechanical arm gleaming in the dim light. "Stay sharp," she called out, her voice steady. "We've trained for this. We've prayed for this. Today, we stand not for ourselves but for the One who called us here."

Wheels rolled into place, his crossbow ready. "They've got numbers, but we've got something they'll never have."

Annabeth moved among the ranks, her presence a calming force. She stopped beside Noah, who adjusted the grip on his spear. "Are you ready?" she asked.

He nodded, though his voice betrayed his nerves. "Ready as I'll ever be."

Annabeth touched his arm, her voice low. "We're not fighting this alone, Noah. Remember that."

The *Chain Breakers* moved into formation, their line tight, their shields raised. The sky above them darkened, swirling with storm clouds that seemed to mirror the tension below. Across the battlefield, Roland's forces began to march, their rhythmic steps like thunder rolling across the earth.

But as the oppressive noise grew louder, a single voice rose above it.

It was Colt. He stepped forward, his shoulders squared, his head held high. He raised his voice, clear and unwavering, and began to sing:

"One voice crying in the wilderness,
One voice proclaiming righteousness;
One man doing what he's called to do,
One man faithful and true."

The *Chain Breakers* stilled, their heads turning toward Colt as his song filled the air. The words carried across the battlefield, strong and unbroken, cutting through the darkness like a blade of light.

"One voice mightier than a thousand swords,
Calling out prepare ye the way of the Lord;
He that is coming is much greater than me,
I will gladly His servant be."

The sound of marching faltered. Even Roland's forces paused, confusion flickering among their ranks. The Anti-Christ's gaze snapped toward the *Chain Breakers*, his expression twisting with disdain.

But Colt didn't stop. His voice grew stronger, his words ringing with faith and defiance:

"One voice crying in the wilderness,
One voice proclaiming righteousness;
One man doing what he's called to do,
One man faithful and true."

Annabeth felt a lump rise in her throat as she joined in, her voice blending with Colt's:

"Then one day John saw with his own eyes,
He of Whom he had prophesied;
The Lamb of God had made His own choice,
To be baptized by the faithful voice."

One by one, the *Chain Breakers* took up the song, their voices lifting in unison. The melody spread through the ranks like wildfire, a defiant hymn that rose above the darkness.

"One voice crying in the wilderness,
Just one voice proclaiming righteousness;
One man doing what he's called to do,
One man faithful and true."

The oppressive weight of the enemy's presence seemed to lessen, the shadows retreating as the song grew louder. The ground beneath their feet seemed to steady, and the winds shifted, carrying the hymn across the battlefield.

On the opposing side, Roland's face twisted in fury. He turned to the Anti-Christ, his voice sharp. "Silence them!"

But the song only grew stronger.

"Yes, one voice crying in the wilderness,
One voice proclaiming righteousness;
One man doing what he's called to do,
One man faithful and true."

As the final notes of the song echoed into the stillness, the *Chain Breakers* stood taller, their hearts steeled by the power of their unity and faith. Across the battlefield, the Anti-Christ's army stirred uneasily, their confidence shaken.

Emmalyn stepped forward, her voice ringing out over the silence. "This battle isn't yours, Roland. It never was. We stand here today, not for ourselves, but for the King of Kings. You can't win against Him."

Annabeth raised her hand, pointing toward the storm-laden sky. "He's coming. And when He does, your darkness will be gone forever."

The Anti-Christ's eyes narrowed, his voice a low growl that rippled with power. "Then let us see if your faith can withstand the fire."

With a roar, Roland's army surged forward, the ground trembling beneath their charge. But the *Chain Breakers* didn't falter. They stood firm, their faith unshaken, their hearts ready for what was to come.

The battle had begun.

Onward, Christian Soldiers

The storm clouds above churned as the two armies faced each other across the barren expanse. The air crackled with tension, every breath heavy with the anticipation of battle. The Chain Breakers stood firm, their formation steady despite the overwhelming force gathered against them. Each warrior gripped their weapon tightly, the resolve in their hearts outweighing the fear in their minds.

Annabeth moved to the front line, her face calm but alight with determination. Emmalyn stood beside her, her sword gleaming even under the dim sky. The sisters exchanged a glance—no words were needed. They both knew what was at stake, and they both knew what they had to do.

Annabeth took a deep breath, stepping forward to address their ranks. "We stand here today for the King of Kings! For truth, for hope, for the light that cannot be overcome! We march forward not in fear, but in faith!"

The Chain Breakers raised their voices in response, a collective cry of courage that echoed across the battlefield.

Emmalyn smirked faintly, rolling her mechanical shoulder. "Let's give them something to march to," she said, her voice low enough for Annabeth alone to hear.

Annabeth nodded and raised her voice. It began soft, but each note carried strength, and soon her words rang out clearly:

"Onward, Christian soldiers,
Marching as to war,
With the cross of Jesus,
Going on before."

Emmalyn grinned, her voice joining Annabeth's, deep and powerful, giving the cadence a commanding rhythm.

"Christ, the royal Master,
Leads against the foe;
Forward into battle,
See His banners go!"

The Chain Breakers took up the song as they began to move, their boots striking the ground in time with the cadence. Their voices rose in unison, a hymn of defiance against the darkness before them.

"Onward, Christian soldiers,
Marching as to war,
With the cross of Jesus,
Going on before."

The sound of their voices carried across the battlefield, slicing through the oppressive air like a blade of light. The rhythm of their march was steady and unyielding, their faith woven into every word.

Across the field, Roland's forces paused for a moment, their advance faltering as the song reached their ears. Confusion flickered in their ranks, the confidence they had carried moments before wavering under the weight of the Chain Breakers' unity.

But the Chain Breakers didn't stop. They pressed forward, their song growing louder:

"Like a mighty army

Moves the church of God;
Brothers, we are treading
Where the saints have trod."

The storm above seemed to boil with fury, lightning splitting the sky as the Anti-Christ raised his hand, his voice booming over the chaos. "Silence them!"

But no command could break the Chain Breakers' resolve. Their march continued, unwavering, as their voices soared:

"We are not divided,
All one body we,
One in hope and doctrine,
One in charity."

The two armies drew closer, the ground trembling beneath the charge of Roland's forces. Yet the Chain Breakers held their formation, their song ringing out like the tolling of a bell in the darkness:

"Onward, Christian soldiers,
Marching as to war,
With the cross of Jesus,
Going on before!"

Annabeth's voice carried above the others, strong and clear. "Forward! For the King of Kings!"

Emmalyn raised her sword high, her own voice fierce. "For the light that never fails!"

The Chain Breakers surged forward as one, their song rising above the clash of steel and the roar of thunder. Each step, each word, carried a faith that no enemy could overcome.

The battle had begun, and the Chain Breakers marched not for their own victory, but for the One who had already won.

The Battle Hymn

The battlefield was chaos. The Chain Breakers fought with everything they had, their weapons clashing against the dark horde. Each strike they landed was a testament to their determination, but the enemy seemed endless, their numbers overwhelming.

Annabeth darted through the fray, her sword in one hand, her shield in the other. Around her, her comrades pushed back the tide of darkness, their faces etched with pain and exhaustion. A few had fallen but refused to stay down, dragging themselves back into the fight with unrelenting resolve.

Annabeth could see fear creeping into their eyes, the weight of the enemy's sheer numbers threatening to crush their spirits. She knew they needed more than weapons to win this battle—they needed hope.

She climbed onto a fallen piece of rubble, her voice piercing through the chaos:

"My hope is built on nothing less
Than Jesus' blood and righteousness;
I dare not trust the sweetest frame,
But wholly lean on Jesus' name."

The soldiers nearest to her turned, their gazes lifting toward the sound. Her voice rose, steady and sure, carrying across the battlefield:

"On Christ, the solid Rock, I stand;
All other ground is sinking sand,
All other ground is sinking sand."

Emmalyn, locked in a fierce duel with a towering enemy, heard her sister's voice and felt her heart lift. She swung her sword with renewed strength, the mechanical arm lending her power beyond her human limits. She parried a blow and joined the hymn, her voice bold and unyielding:

"When darkness veils His lovely face,
I rest on His unchanging grace;
In every high and stormy gale,
My anchor holds within the veil."

The Chain Breakers took up the hymn one by one, their voices rising above the din of battle.

Wheels, despite a deep cut on his arm, rolled forward, his crossbow firing into the enemy ranks. He sang with a voice as unshakable as his aim:

"On Christ, the solid Rock, I stand;
All other ground is sinking sand,
All other ground is sinking sand."

Noah, blood dripping from a wound on his temple, staggered but found his footing. He drove his spear into an advancing foe and turned to rally those near him. "Keep singing!" he shouted. "Let them hear us!"

The hymn spread like wildfire. Even Kelli, leaning heavily on her axe after a brutal strike, lifted her voice in harmony with the others. The Chain Breakers moved as one, their song pushing back the despair that sought to overwhelm them.

"His oath, His covenant, His blood,
Support me in the whelming flood;

When all around my soul gives way,
He then is all my hope and stay."

The dark army faltered. The power of the hymn was undeniable, a light that pierced even the deepest shadow. Roland's forces hesitated, their lines wavering under the strength of the Chain Breakers' unity and faith.

Above the battlefield, the storm clouds churned, lightning flashing in jagged streaks across the sky. The Anti-Christ, seated atop his black steed, roared with fury. "They will not win! Crush them!"

But no command could silence the Chain Breakers. Their voices only grew stronger:

"On Christ, the solid Rock, I stand;
All other ground is sinking sand,
All other ground is sinking sand."

Annabeth raised her sword high, her voice carrying the final verse:

"When He shall come with trumpet sound,
Oh, may I then in Him be found;
Dressed in His righteousness alone,
Faultless to stand before the throne."

The Chain Breakers surged forward, their hymn a weapon as powerful as their blades. The enemy reeled under the combined force of their faith and determination, their once-imposing ranks thrown into disarray.

"On Christ, the solid Rock, I stand;
All other ground is sinking sand,
All other ground is sinking sand."

As the last note rang out, the Chain Breakers pressed the advantage, their spirits lifted, their hope unshaken. The enemy might have numbers, but the Chain Breakers had something far greater—faith in the unyielding power of the One who stood with them.

The battle raged on, but the Chain Breakers would not falter. Their song, their unity, and their hope carried them forward, a light in the darkness that refused to be extinguished.

Unmeasured Grace

The battle raged on, but something extraordinary began to ripple through the chaos. The Chain Breakers sang as they fought, their voices unwavering even as the storm above raged and the enemy pressed harder. Their hymns carried not just strength but a power that could not be seen—faith that cut through fear, light that pierced the deepest darkness.

"Amazing grace, how sweet the sound,
That saved a wretch like me.
I once was lost, but now am found,
Was blind, but now I see."

Annabeth's voice rang out above the noise, her sword flashing as she parried an enemy's strike. Her song was infectious, and the Chain Breakers sang with her, their voices lifting as one.

Across the battlefield, the enemy faltered. Those who had been so certain of victory now hesitated, confusion and something deeper flickering in their eyes.

One of Roland's soldiers—a young man with a torn black tabard—stumbled back from the front lines. His weapon fell from his hands as he stared at the Chain Breakers, his face pale. "How... how can you keep singing?" he shouted, his voice breaking. "How can you fight and still have hope?"

Annabeth turned toward him, her gaze steady. She lowered her sword, stepping forward even as the battle raged around her. "We sing because we have faith," she said, her voice carrying. "We fight because we know this battle is not ours alone. And we hope because of God's unmeasured grace."

The soldier fell to his knees, tears streaming down his face. "What is that grace? How can you have it? I've done things... terrible things."

Emmalyn, blood-streaked but unbowed, came to stand beside her sister. She looked at the soldier, her mechanical hand resting lightly on her sword. "None of us are here because we're perfect," she said. "We're here because we're forgiven. That's the power of grace—it's not about what we've done. It's about what He's done for us."

More soldiers began to drop their weapons, their faces filled with a mix of fear and yearning. One of them called out, "What do we do? How can we find what you have?"

Annabeth knelt in the blood-stained dirt, meeting the gaze of the first soldier. "You turn away from the darkness," she said simply. "You confess what's in your heart. And you let His grace cover you."

The young man's voice shook. "How? How do I do that?"

"Pray," Annabeth said, reaching out her hand. "Ask Him to forgive you. He's already waiting. His grace is unmeasured, greater than anything you've done."

The soldier hesitated, then clasped her hand. He bowed his head, his voice trembling as he began to pray.

Around them, more of the enemy laid down their weapons, their faces turned toward the Chain Breakers. The hymn continued, softer now, but no less powerful:

"'Twas grace that taught my heart to fear,
And grace my fears relieved;
How precious did that grace appear,
The hour I first believed."

Kelli, limping but still upright, moved among the surrendered soldiers, her axe lowered. "This isn't just a fight against flesh and blood," she said to one of them. "It's a battle for your soul. And you're not too far gone."

Wheels, his crossbow resting on his lap, added his voice to the chorus, the rough timbre of his song filled with conviction:

"Through many dangers, toils, and snares,
I have already come;
'Tis grace hath brought me safe thus far,
And grace will lead me home."

The battlefield began to shift. Where there had been chaos, there was now an undeniable sense of peace settling over parts of the plain. Roland's forces weren't just faltering—they were breaking, not from fear but from a longing for something greater than the darkness they had served.

The Anti-Christ's voice roared across the battlefield, his rage shaking the ground. "You think you can save them? They are mine!"

But Annabeth stood firm, her voice rising in response. "They belong to Him, and His grace is stronger than your chains!"

The Chain Breakers gathered closer, their formation tightening as they protected those who had surrendered. Their song rose again, filling the air with a truth that could not be silenced:

"The Lord has promised good to me,
His word my hope secures;

He will my shield and portion be,
As long as life endures."

As the hymn echoed across the battlefield, more of the enemy fell to their knees, crying out for the grace they now knew was real. And in that moment, the Chain Breakers knew they were not just fighting a battle—they were part of a victory far greater than themselves.

The power of unmeasured grace was turning the tide, one soul at a time.

The Fierce Push

The lull in the battle was brief. Roland's forces, rattled by the defections and the Chain Breakers' unwavering faith, reassembled with renewed fury. The Anti-Christ, his dark armor glinting beneath the storm-filled sky, raised his hand, and the ground trembled. Shadows writhed around him, unnatural and menacing, as if the very earth obeyed his command.

"You think your songs and your faith will save you?" his voice boomed, unnatural and deep, resonating across the battlefield. "You are nothing but dust before me. Watch as your hope crumbles!"

At his signal, Roland's remaining forces surged forward, their ranks tightening into disciplined waves of destruction. Their movements were sharper, their strikes fiercer, as though they'd been infused with an unholy power.

Annabeth felt the ground shake beneath her feet as the enemy charged. She turned to her comrades, her voice sharp but steady. "Hold the line! We've faced worse before. Stand together!"

Emmalyn raised her sword, her mechanical arm gleaming with a faint, golden light as it caught the weak sunlight breaking through the storm. "Chain Breakers!" she roared. "Don't give an inch!"

The two sides clashed again, the sound of metal on metal deafening. The enemy came with a fury that was almost overwhelming, their weapons striking with unnatural precision. Chain Breakers fell under the onslaught, but those who could still move fought on, refusing to yield.

Noah blocked a heavy strike with his spear, gritting his teeth as he pushed back. "They're stronger," he shouted over the chaos. "It's like they've been unleashed!"

Kelli, her axe cleaving through an enemy's shield, nodded grimly. "Then we fight harder. We didn't come this far to back down!"

Even as they fought, the Chain Breakers continued to sing, their hymns a shield against the despair creeping at the edges of their minds. But now, their voices were strained, their strength waning under the relentless pressure of the enemy's assault.

Annabeth swung her sword, felling an attacker before turning to Emmalyn. "We need something more," she said, her voice tight with urgency.

Emmalyn's jaw clenched as she drove back an enemy with a powerful strike. "Then we give them everything we've got," she said.

The Anti-Christ rode forward, his dark steed trampling the ground as he raised a massive blade that seemed to pulse with shadow. "Destroy them!" he roared, pointing his sword toward the Chain Breakers.

A fresh wave of darkness swept over the battlefield, and Roland's forces surged again, their ferocity redoubling.

Wheels, still holding his position despite a wound to his side, fired a bolt into the chest of an advancing soldier. "They just keep coming!" he shouted.

"We'll hold!" Annabeth cried, raising her voice above the din. She stepped forward, planting herself firmly in the center of the line. Lifting her voice, she began to sing again, her hymn defiant in the face of the darkness:

"Stand up, stand up for Jesus,
Ye soldiers of the cross;
Lift high His royal banner,
It must not suffer loss."

Her voice cut through the chaos, and one by one, the Chain Breakers joined in, their words an anchor amidst the storm of battle.

"From victory unto victory,
His army shall He lead,
Till every foe is vanquished,
And Christ is Lord indeed."

The hymn strengthened their resolve, giving them the will to push back against the relentless onslaught. Emmalyn fought her way to Annabeth's side, her sword slashing through the enemy ranks. She added her voice to the hymn, her words ringing with determination:

"Stand up, stand up for Jesus,
The strife will not be long;
This day the noise of battle,
The next the victor's song."

But the enemy's ferocity did not wane. The Anti-Christ's dark power seemed to fuel his army, driving them to fight harder, faster, more ruthlessly.

Annabeth looked around at her comrades, their faces strained but determined. She knew they were holding on by faith alone. Turning her gaze toward the sky, she whispered a prayer, her words lost in the noise of the battle but heard by the One she called upon.

"Lord, give us strength. Not for ourselves, but for Your glory. We trust in Your grace to carry us through."

Her heart steadied, and she turned back to the fight, her voice lifting the hymn once more.

The Chain Breakers sang louder, their voices defiant as they fought on. The battle was fierce, and many fell wounded, but none surrendered. Their hope, their faith, and their resolve burned brighter even as the darkness pressed harder against them.

The Anti-Christ, his eyes blazing with fury, watched as the Chain Breakers continued to stand. He raised his blade high, summoning a fresh wave of shadow, his voice dripping with malice. "You will break, and your faith will die with you!"

But the Chain Breakers answered not with fear, but with song. Their hymn rose above the battlefield, a beacon of light in the darkest hour:

"To him that overcometh
A crown of life shall be;
He with the King of glory
Shall reign eternally."

The battle raged on, but the Chain Breakers stood firm, knowing that their strength came not from themselves, but from the grace of the One who called them to stand.

Devil's Gonna Run

As the sun dipped below the horizon, the battlefield fell into an uneasy stillness. The echoes of battle faded into the cool night air, leaving both armies to retreat and regroup. Fires dotted the Chain Breakers' camp, their flickering light casting long shadows on weary faces.

Emmalyn sat on a boulder near the edge of the camp, her sword resting across her knees. She gazed out at the battlefield, where broken weapons and scattered armor marked the day's struggle. Her mechanical arm whirred softly as she flexed it, ensuring it would be ready for what was to come.

Annabeth approached, her steps light but deliberate. She carried a waterskin, which she handed to her sister before sitting beside her.

"You should rest," Annabeth said quietly. "Tomorrow will be worse."

Emmalyn took a long drink before wiping her mouth with the back of her hand. "Rest when it's over," she replied.

Annabeth sighed but didn't argue. Instead, she looked out at the dark horizon, where the enemy's campfires glimmered like distant stars. "Do you think they're as tired as we are?"

"Maybe," Emmalyn said, her voice low. "But they're not going to stop. And neither are we."

Annabeth placed a hand on her sister's shoulder. "You were incredible today. They're looking to you, Em. You've given them courage."

Emmalyn's gaze remained fixed ahead, her voice soft. "I just hope it's enough."

"It will be," Annabeth said firmly. "Because it's not just us out there. He's with us. Always."

The sisters sat in silence for a moment before Annabeth stood, her hand brushing Emmalyn's shoulder briefly. "Try to sleep, Em. We'll need every bit of strength tomorrow."

As the night deepened, the Chain Breakers rested fitfully, their dreams filled with visions of the battle still to come. Across the field, Roland's forces did the same, their leaders plotting and strategizing under the Anti-Christ's watchful gaze.

The first light of dawn broke over the battlefield, painting the scarred earth in muted gold. The Chain Breakers rose early, their movements methodical as they prepared for another day of battle. Armor was repaired, weapons were sharpened, and prayers were whispered into the cool morning air.

Emmalyn stood at the front of the formation, her eyes scanning the horizon. The enemy was already assembling, their dark banners rippling in the breeze. The weight of the moment pressed heavily on her chest, but she took a steadying breath, drawing strength from the faith that had carried them this far.

As the Chain Breakers began to march forward, Emmalyn's voice broke the stillness, strong and defiant:

"The devil thought he had a hold of me,
He told so many lies that I believed.
Got too weak to carry on,
I thought that I was too far gone."

The familiar melody filled the air, and heads turned toward her. A few weary smiles spread through the ranks as her voice carried on, bold and unyielding.

"But then I heard a voice from Calvary,
And now I'm singing, no more shackles on my feet!
The devil's gotta run."

Annabeth joined her, her voice blending with her sister's as the song grew louder.

"He's been telling me to run,
But I'm not running out of steam, no.
The devil's gotta run."

The Chain Breakers picked up the chorus, their voices ringing across the plain. Their steps fell in time with the rhythm of the song, their confidence growing with each word.

"Oh, he's been running to the darkness,
But the darkness ain't no place to hide.
The devil's gotta run."

Even as the enemy's lines approached, the Chain Breakers' song rose above the clamor, a defiant declaration of faith and victory. Emmalyn led them, her voice unwavering, her mechanical arm gleaming in the morning light as she raised her sword.

"Get behind me, Satan,
No more fear and no more shame!
My debt's been paid, I'm free in Jesus' name!"

The enemy hesitated. Their dark ranks wavered under the power of the Chain Breakers' united voices. The Anti-Christ rode to the front of his army, his eyes blazing with fury as the song reached him.

"Silence them!" he bellowed, his voice echoing like thunder.

But the Chain Breakers were unstoppable. Their voices soared as they drew closer, their faith radiating like a shield against the enemy's darkness.

"The devil thought he had a hold of me,
But now I'm free, I'm free indeed!
The devil's gotta run!"

The battle was about to begin anew, but the Chain Breakers moved forward with unwavering faith, their song a banner of hope and defiance. Emmalyn's voice led the charge, her words cutting through the tension like a blade of light:

"The devil's gotta run."

The Unveiling

The battlefield grew still, a heavy silence descending as the clouds above parted. A light so brilliant and pure poured through the sky, shattering the darkness that had covered the earth. Both armies stopped in their tracks, their gazes lifted in awe and fear.

The Anti-Christ, sitting atop his black steed, narrowed his eyes at the light, his face twisted with rage. "No. This cannot be," he hissed, his voice trembling with fury. "This is not part of the plan."

The light continued to grow, and from within it emerged a figure on a white horse, radiant and commanding. His presence overwhelmed the battlefield, as though the very heavens themselves had come to witness His arrival. His robe shone with the brilliance of the sun, and His face, though serene, bore the authority of eternity.

In His right hand, He held a sharp sword—its blade glinting with divine power. But what truly caught the eye were the words inscribed upon it, in letters that burned with truth and might:

"KING OF KINGS AND LORD OF LORDS."

The Chain Breakers fell to their knees, their voices caught in their throats as they beheld the one they had long hoped for. Annabeth's eyes filled with tears, her heart swelling with the realization of what they were witnessing. "It's Him," she whispered, awe and joy in her voice. "It's Jesus."

The Anti-Christ's forces, once so sure of their victory, now faltered. Roland turned to the Anti-Christ, his voice strained. "What is this? This isn't possible. We were promised eternal victory!"

The Anti-Christ's face contorted with rage, his hands gripping his dark blade tightly. "Press forward! The battle is not over!"

But even as he shouted, doubt began to seep into his ranks. Some soldiers stood frozen in place, their faces pale as they looked toward the Rider. Others began to drop their weapons, their bodies trembling with fear.

The Rider on the white horse, Jesus Himself, moved forward. The ground seemed to tremble beneath His horse's hooves, as though the earth itself recognized His authority. The sword He held gleamed brighter with each passing moment, the words on the blade burning with an undeniable truth:

"KING OF KINGS AND LORD OF LORDS."

Annabeth, tears streaming down her face, rose to her feet, her voice trembling but strong. "He is here. The King of Kings has come!"

The Chain Breakers, their hearts lifted with renewed strength, began to sing. Their voices rose in unison, a hymn of triumph and faith:

"Crown Him with many crowns,
The Lamb upon His throne;

Hark! how the heavenly anthem drowns
All music but its own."

The angelic host appeared, a vast, uncountable army of heavenly warriors, their swords drawn and gleaming. Their voices joined with the Chain Breakers' in a song of victory, filling the air with power and hope.

"Awake, my soul, and sing
Of Him who died for thee,
And hail Him as thy matchless King
Through all eternity."

The Anti-Christ roared in fury, his sword raised high as he ordered his forces to charge. "Attack! Destroy them!"

But his army hesitated. The sight of the Rider—the King—was too much. Many dropped to their knees in fear, unable to face the One who now stood in judgment.

The Chain Breakers, emboldened by the presence of their Savior, pressed forward. Emmalyn raised her sword, her voice joining the hymn as they advanced. "For the King! For the King of Kings!"

Jesus, the Rider, did not raise His sword in anger but in authority. His presence alone was enough to send a wave of fear through the Anti-Christ's ranks. His sword, still gleaming with the inscription *"KING OF KINGS AND LORD OF LORDS,"* was a declaration that all power on earth, under the earth, and in the heavens was His.

The final battle had begun, but the victory had already been secured. The King had come, and His army would not be defeated. The Chain Breakers stood firm, knowing that with the King before them, no power could stand against them.

The Battle of Armageddon

The earth itself seemed to tremble as the armies gathered for the final confrontation. On one side, the Chain Breakers stood united, their hearts full of faith, their swords gleaming with resolve. Behind them, an uncountable host of angels filled the sky, their presence overwhelming. And at the front, mounted on a brilliant white horse, rode Jesus—the King of Kings and Lord of Lords—His sword raised high, the words *"KING OF KINGS AND LORD OF LORDS"* gleaming in the light.

Across the battlefield, the Anti-Christ's forces stood ready. Their dark armor seemed to absorb the light around them, and the ground beneath their feet pulsed with the darkness they served. The Anti-Christ himself rode at the front, his black steed galloping with unholy fury. The earth crackled with energy as he raised his blade toward the heavens.

"Today, we crush them," he snarled, his voice filled with venom. "The King will fall, and I will reign!"

The battle was about to begin.

With a roar, the Anti-Christ's army surged forward, a wave of dark warriors crashing toward the Chain Breakers. The sound of their footsteps was like thunder, a terrifying crescendo of destruction. But the Chain Breakers stood firm, their voices rising in a mighty chorus, a declaration of defiance against the darkness.

"Onward, Christian soldiers,
Marching as to war,
With the cross of Jesus,
Going on before."

The hymn rang out, filling the air with light, and the heavens seemed to respond. Angels descended like a storm of fire and light, their swords flashing as they joined the Chain Breakers in their charge. The battle for Armageddon had begun.

The Anti-Christ's forces met the first wave of angels, and the air filled with the sound of clashing steel. The ground shook as the two armies collided, the sheer force of their impact sending shockwaves through the earth.

Emmalyn swung her sword, cutting down an enemy soldier, her eyes locked onto the Anti-Christ. "For the King!" she shouted, her voice fierce.

Beside her, Annabeth fought with unyielding faith, her shield raised as she deflected a strike. "We are not alone!" she cried, rallying those around her.

The forces of darkness pressed harder, but the Chain Breakers stood strong, their faith and unity an unbreakable shield. They fought with the strength of God's grace, knowing that their victory was assured, that the King who rode before them would never be defeated.

In the distance, the Anti-Christ bellowed, his rage echoing across the battlefield. "You think you can defeat me? I am the ruler of this world!" He raised his dark sword, and a wave of dark energy surged forward, crashing into the Chain Breakers like a tidal wave.

But Jesus, His presence filling the battlefield with light, raised His sword high. The darkness recoiled at His approach. "It is finished," He declared, His voice resonating through the very air, a proclamation of victory over all that had come against Him.

With a single sweep of His sword, the darkness was shattered. The Anti-Christ's forces staggered, their fear palpable. They had never known an enemy like this—an enemy who could not be defeated.

The Chain Breakers, emboldened by the King's presence, surged forward. Their voices grew louder, their hymn stronger, as they pressed into the heart of the enemy's forces.

"Stand up, stand up for Jesus,
Ye soldiers of the cross;
Lift high His royal banner,
It must not suffer loss."

The Anti-Christ, seeing his army falter, raised his blade in one last, desperate attempt to turn the tide. "Fight! Fight for your master!" he cried, but his words were drowned out by the sound of the Chain Breakers' song, their voices louder than the clash of swords, their faith stronger than any force he could summon.

Roland, standing beside the Anti-Christ, faltered, his eyes wide with fear. "This... this is not possible," he whispered. "They are too strong."

The Anti-Christ's eyes narrowed in hatred, and he charged toward Jesus, his dark sword raised high. "I will destroy you!" he screamed.

But before he could reach Jesus, a wave of light surged forward from the heavenly host, knocking him back. The Anti-Christ tumbled to the ground, his blade falling from his hand.

The moment he hit the ground, the light around him intensified, encasing him in a brilliant cage of divine power. He writhed in fury, his cries of rage filling the air, but he could not escape.

Jesus rode forward, His sword gleaming with righteous power. He raised it high, and the words *"KING OF KINGS AND LORD OF LORDS"* burned even brighter.

The Anti-Christ looked up in fear, his voice a mere whisper. "No... not now..."

But with a single swing of the sword, Jesus brought the battle to its end. The Anti-Christ was cast down, his reign of darkness broken forever.

The armies of the Chain Breakers and the heavenly host surged forward in a wave of light, sweeping through the remaining forces of darkness. The battle was won.

As the dust settled and the last of the enemy was scattered, the Chain Breakers stood together, their voices rising in a triumphant song of praise:

"Hallelujah, for the Lord God omnipotent reigneth!
Hallelujah, hallelujah, hallelujah, Amen!"

Jesus, His sword still gleaming, rode forward, His presence like a beacon of peace in the aftermath of the battle. The earth had been cleansed, the darkness defeated, and the King of Kings had claimed His victory.

The Chain Breakers knelt, their hearts overflowing with gratitude and awe. They had fought with faith, and by the grace of God, they had won.

The King had come, and His reign would last forever.

The New Kingdom

The earth lay still, the aftermath of battle and destruction replaced by an overwhelming sense of peace. The skies, once heavy with dark clouds, had cleared, and the golden light of Jesus' presence bathed the land, as if the heavens themselves were rejoicing. The victory of Armageddon was not just a victory over darkness—it was the beginning of a new chapter in creation.

Jesus, His face radiant with glory, stood amidst the Chain Breakers, His sword held high, the words *"KING OF KINGS AND LORD OF LORDS"* still etched upon it, gleaming with divine power. Around Him, the vast host of angels stood in formation, their faces calm, their swords still raised in silent victory.

The earth had changed. Where there had once been barren lands, now green fields and blooming flowers stretched out in every direction. The mountains, once scarred and broken, were now covered in lush forests, and rivers that had run dry with judgment flowed once again with fresh, pure waters.

Annabeth stood at the front of the Chain Breakers, her heart swelling with awe as she looked out at the transformed land. "It's all so beautiful," she whispered. "It's like the world has come alive again."

Emmalyn, standing beside her, nodded. Her mechanical arm gleamed in the sunlight as she touched her chest, her heart beating with a joy she had never known. "It's more than beauty," she said softly. "It's the world as it was always meant to be."

Jesus turned toward them, His gaze filled with love. "Behold, I make all things new," He said, His voice gentle but filled with power. His words echoed through the land, a declaration that the curse of sin had been broken, and the earth had been restored.

The Chain Breakers looked around them, their faces shining with gratitude. They had fought the battle of Armageddon, and now they saw the result of their faithfulness: a world renewed, a kingdom established where peace reigned and the righteous would live in harmony with God forever.

The landscape had been cleansed. Where once evil had corrupted the earth, now it was restored, reflecting the purity and beauty of God's original creation.

Jesus stepped forward, His presence calming the hearts of all who stood before Him. "The time of suffering is over. The wicked are no more. And those who have followed Me will dwell in peace, in joy, and in eternal fellowship with Me."

Annabeth's voice was filled with awe as she looked toward Jesus. "This is the kingdom we've been waiting for. This is the world You promised."

Emmalyn looked at her sister, a smile breaking across her face. "It's real. All of it. The promises, the hope. It's all true."

Jesus smiled at them, His eyes full of love. "You have fought the good fight, and now you will live in the peace that I have brought. A thousand years of rest, of renewal, of harmony with the Father. No more pain. No more sorrow. No more death."

And with that, a thousand years of peace began. The earth was not just restored, it was transformed into the perfect place for the righteous to live. Every corner of the land was filled with light, with life, and with the peace of God's presence. The curse had been lifted, and humanity now stood in the eternal light of the Creator, walking in the harmony that had been lost in the Garden of Eden.

The Chain Breakers, those who had remained faithful, stood in awe as the world around them was reborn. They were not just witnesses to the change—they were part of it, living in the new creation that had been established. Their hearts were full, their minds at peace, for they knew that this was the world they had been fighting for, a world where God's love reigned supreme, and where no evil could ever touch again.

The land was clean, the skies clear, and the people—those who had accepted Jesus—were united in harmony, living in fellowship with one another and with God. This was not just the beginning of a thousand years of peace; this was the start of something eternal, something perfect.

As the sun set on the first day of the new kingdom, the Chain Breakers stood together, their hearts full of gratitude. They had fought for this day, and now they saw the fulfillment of God's promises. The old order had passed away, and everything had been made new.

For the next thousand years, peace would reign, and the righteous would live in the presence of their Savior, in a world that had been renewed, cleansed, and transformed—just as it had always been meant to be.

Life in His Kingdom

The world, now made new, basked under the eternal light of Jesus' reign. The once-barren lands had blossomed into a paradise—lush fields, vibrant forests, and crystal-clear rivers stretched as far as the eye could see. The very air seemed to hum with peace, the atmosphere thick with the presence of God's glory. The earth, healed and restored, radiated life in a way it never had before.

Life under the reign of Jesus was unlike anything the world had known. The people who lived there—those who had remained faithful, those who had chosen to follow Christ—now lived in perfect harmony with God and with each other. There were no more divisions, no more strife, no more fear. Every need was met, every heart at rest.

Annabeth walked through the gardens of the new city, the streets lined with trees bearing fruit of every kind. She paused by a flowing river, its waters crystal clear, sparkling under the brilliant sun. The sound of birds singing echoed in the air as the landscape flourished.

"It's everything we dreamed of," she said softly to Emmalyn, who stood beside her, gazing out over the horizon.

"It's everything we fought for," Emmalyn replied, her voice thick with emotion. She turned to her sister. "It's more than I ever imagined. There's peace here. Real peace."

The world was alive in ways that couldn't be described by words alone. The earth itself seemed to breathe, its wounds healed by the touch of the Creator. The oceans sparkled in the sunlight, and the skies were a never-ending canvas of blue, streaked with soft, golden clouds. There were no more storms of destruction, no more droughts or famines.

In the heart of the kingdom stood the city, radiant and full of life. Its walls were made of precious stones, shining like diamonds, and its gates were made of pearls. The streets were paved with gold, but the gold was not the object of beauty—it was the peace and harmony that filled every corner of the city. People lived freely, without fear of disease, injury, or death. There was no need for hospitals, no need for warriors or defense. The war had been won, and the peace was everlasting.

In this new world, there were no longer any differences based on status, wealth, or race. Every person was united under the reign of Jesus. All lived as one family, brothers and sisters in Christ, working together for the common good. People no longer fought for resources or power; all needs were met in abundance, and generosity flowed freely between all. Every person had what they needed, and more.

Emmalyn smiled as she watched a group of children play in the meadow nearby, their laughter light and carefree. Their lives were full of joy, unburdened by the struggles that once plagued the earth. "Do you think they'll ever know what it was like before?" she asked softly.

Annabeth shook her head. "No. They'll only know peace. They'll only know joy and harmony with God. And they'll grow up in a world that will never change—never fall into darkness again."

As the days passed, the people of the new kingdom lived in harmony, following the example of Jesus, whose teachings were not only words but the foundation of their every action. He was not a distant ruler in this kingdom. He was with His people, walking among them, talking with them, guiding them with gentle wisdom. There was no hierarchy, no need for power or dominion, for everyone was equal in His sight.

The days began to blend together—each one filled with worship, with work, with rest. People would gather in the great open fields to hear Jesus teach, His words full of life and wisdom, and they would spend their days in fellowship and service to one another. There were no burdens, no toil that could not be eased, no work that was ever too much.

Annabeth and Emmalyn walked side by side through the city, gazing at the beauty that surrounded them. They marveled at the trees that bore fruit in every season, the animals that roamed freely without fear, the rivers that never ran dry.

"This," Emmalyn said, "this is what life was always meant to be."

Annabeth nodded. "It is. No more pain. No more struggle. Just... peace. The world has been made whole again."

As they walked, they passed people who were busy rebuilding, creating, living fully in the presence of the King. There were no more sicknesses or diseases to heal, but people still cared for each other, lifting each other up in love and unity. Everyone shared their talents, their gifts, to serve one another in ways that brought joy, not obligation. Families lived together in joy, raising children in the knowledge of God's love and faithfulness.

And in the evenings, when the sun set in perfect hues of pink and gold, people would gather to praise. The skies above the city would light up with the glow of countless stars, each one a reminder of the Creator's care for every detail, every life. Their praises echoed across the land, a constant and beautiful song to the One who had made it all possible.

Emmalyn turned to Annabeth as the evening settled in. "Do you think we'll ever stop marveling at this?" she asked.

Annabeth smiled, a peaceful calm settling over her heart. "No. We'll never stop marveling. And we'll never stop worshiping. Because He made it all possible. He is the reason we are here, and He will be with us forever."

The thousand years of peace had begun, and under the reign of Jesus, the world was everything it was meant to be—perfect, unbroken, and filled with the unending love of the Creator. There was no sorrow, no pain, no more death. Only life, only peace, only love. And the promise that this world—this new kingdom—would never fade. It was eternal, just as He had always promised.

The Final Victory

The thousand years had passed in peace. Under the reign of Jesus, the world had been transformed into a paradise, a reflection of the perfect harmony that existed in the heart of God. For a millennium, the faithful had lived without fear or pain, the earth itself healed and flourishing. The nations lived in unity, their hearts devoted to God, and all creation rejoiced in the eternal presence of the King.

But even in this perfect kingdom, a time would come when the final test would be faced. The end of the Millennium was near, and the unthinkable began to unfold.

In the quiet peace of the Kingdom, the world did not know that Satan—bound for a thousand years in the abyss—was about to be released. The forces of darkness, once vanquished, began to stir once again as the ancient enemy was freed from his prison. For the first time in a millennium, the earth trembled at his awakening. His heart filled with hatred and pride, and the seed of rebellion began to grow in the darkness of his soul.

Satan's first act was to seduce the nations. In the peace that had reigned for so long, the hearts of some had grown complacent, forgetting the true reason for the harmony around them. Satan whispered lies into their hearts, stirring up pride, doubt, and a thirst for power. The enemy who had once sought to lead a rebellion in heaven now sought to corrupt the very people who had known peace and love for a thousand years.

With cunning deceit, he gathered the nations once more, stirring them to war. His lies spread like wildfire, and many who had once known the peace of Christ were deceived into believing that they could overthrow the King and claim the earth for themselves.

Emmalyn, standing with Annabeth on a hill overlooking the city, felt a strange stirring in her spirit. "Something's not right," she murmured, her eyes scanning the horizon.

Annabeth, who had seen the faith of God's people remain unshaken for so long, felt the same unease. "I can feel it too. The peace—something is threatening it."

Far below them, the nations had gathered, an army greater than any the earth had seen in the thousand years since Jesus had reigned. They assembled in the valley of decision, preparing to march against the holy city. The enemy had seduced them, promising victory, power, and freedom from God's rule. But they would never understand the truth of what they were doing.

Satan stood at the head of this army, his eyes burning with the desire to overthrow everything that had been established. He had failed before, and he had been bound, but now he sought to deceive and destroy once more.

But as the armies of the world gathered, Jesus, the King of Kings, stood firm in His position of authority. His eyes, full of righteousness, gazed upon the assembled nations. With a voice that could not be ignored, He spoke:

"It is finished."

As the words left His mouth, fire rained down from heaven, consuming the armies of rebellion in an instant. The earth shook, and the armies of the nations were consumed in a blaze of divine fury, their rebellion nothing but ashes before the throne of the King. There was no war, no struggle—just the overwhelming power of God's judgment. The nations had gathered for battle, but their rebellion was crushed without a fight, for it was the fire of heaven that fell upon them.

The Anti-Christ, the deceiver, and his army were no more. They had sought to overthrow God's kingdom, but their rebellion was doomed to failure from the start. In the aftermath, the heavens were silent, and the earth stood still, witnessing the victory of God. Satan was seized, bound once again, and cast into the lake of fire and sulfur—there to remain for eternity, never to deceive or destroy again.

With the forces of evil finally defeated, the earth and heavens began to shift once more. A new chapter in creation began, for the time had come for the ultimate fulfillment of God's plan. The heavens above and the earth below, though once marred and broken by sin, were now ready for their ultimate renewal.

As Satan was thrown into the lake of fire, the world began to change. The old order had passed away. There was no more pain, no more death. No more tears or suffering. The old heaven and the old earth, in all their corrupted form, faded into nothingness, and from their ashes, a new heaven and a new earth emerged.

The air was fresh, filled with the scent of life and peace. The world was not as it had been before; it was something more. Every mountain, every river, every star in the sky reflected the glory of God in perfect harmony. The earth had been made new, without flaw, without sin. No longer would creation groan in waiting for the redemption of the children of God; it had been made whole.

And those who had been faithful, those who had followed Christ through every trial, were now granted immortal bodies. They walked the new earth, free from death, free from decay. They were no longer bound by the limitations of the mortal world, for they had been transformed.

Emmalyn and Annabeth stood together, their eyes wide with wonder as they looked upon the new world. The life they had fought for was now their eternal reality. The new Jerusalem, a city unlike any other, stood before them—its gates made of pearls, its streets paved with gold, shining with the unending glory of God. The light of Christ filled every corner of the city, and the people walked in peace, their hearts full of joy, their lives filled with purpose.

"We're home," Emmalyn said quietly, her voice filled with awe. "It's finally here. The kingdom we've dreamed of."

Annabeth smiled, her eyes shining. "It's perfect. And it's forever."

As they stood in the presence of the King, they knew that this was the final victory. Satan's rebellion had been crushed, and the new heaven and earth were established. The people of God were free, their lives filled with eternal peace, joy, and worship. And the King, the One who had made it all possible, stood at the center of it all, reigning forevermore.

The earth was now as it was always meant to be—perfect, whole, and free from sin. This was the culmination of God's perfect plan, and it would never end. There would be no more sorrow, no more pain. Only life, only light, only love—forever.

www.ingramcontent.com/pod-product-compliance
Lightning Source LLC
LaVergne TN
LVHW040918150826
845672LV00007B/2093

9798230637493